D1201010

GAME FACE

Softball Surprise

by Brigitte Cooper
illustrated by Tim Heitz

Calico

An Imprint of Magic Wagon
abdopublishing.com

For Mom, Dad, Scott, John & Jane: My original and forever favorite cast of characters! —BC

abdopublishing.com

Published by Magic Wagon, a division of ABDO, PO Box 398166, Minneapolis, Minnesota 55439. Copyright © 2018 by Abdo Consulting Group, Inc. International copyrights reserved in all countries. No part of this book may be reproduced in any form without written permission from the publisher. Calico™ is a trademark and logo of Magic Wagon.

Printed in the United States of America, North Mankato, Minnesota.
102017
012018

THIS BOOK CONTAINS RECYCLED MATERIALS

Written by Brigitte Cooper
Illustrated by Tim Heitz
Edited by Megan M. Gunderson
Art Directed by Laura Mitchell

Once again, very special thanks to our content consultant, Scott Lauinger!

Publisher's Cataloging-in-Publication Data

Names: Cooper, Brigitte, author. | Heitz, Tim, illustrator.
Title: Softball surprise / by Brigitte Cooper; illustrated by Tim Heitz.
Description: Minneapolis, Minnesota : Magic Wagon, 2018. | Series: Game face
Summary: Rana Parisi calls the shots as her softball team's catcher, but when she hurts a friend's feelings while planning a surprise birthday party, Rana struggles to keep focused as her team heads to the summer championships and figure out how to repair her friendship.
Identifiers: LCCN 2017946494 | ISBN 9781532130441 (lib.bdg.) | ISBN 9781532131042 (ebook) | ISBN 9781532131349 (Read-to-me ebook)
Subjects: LCSH: Softball--Juvenile fiction. | Friendship--Juvenile fiction. | Emotions--Juvenile fiction. | Self-reliance in adolescence--Juvenile fiction.
Classification: DDC [FIC]--dc23
LC record available at https://lccn.loc.gov/2017946494

TABLE OF CONTENTS

ONE

Bottom of the Ninth

Crack!

The second the softball smacked against the sweet spot of the Louisville slugger, I knew it was a double, if not better. I love the sound of bat connecting with ball, how the shock waves travel down the body of the bat into my hands, zinging my fingers with victory.

Only thing was, I wasn't the batter. I was already on base.

"Run, Rana, run!"

I didn't even hear the cheers from the background. I calmed my mind, took a deep breath, and turned the noise into a quiet hum of energy. It's not often that I get on base. So when I do, I take it very seriously. I'm working on my batting skills. But until they improve, my trips to first base are few and far between.

It was the bottom of the ninth. No outs. My team, the Dodgers, was tied with the Cardinals. One more run would win us the game and clinch our spot in first place at the end of the regular season. A victory we had chased all year long.

As soon as Alana dropped her bat and headed for first, I took off. Rather than watch the softball to see where it landed, I kept my focus on Coach Kim at third base. If I was supposed to keep running, she would let me know.

Sure enough, as I sprinted toward second, Coach Kim waved her arms in a giant circle—the signal to keep running! I rounded second and headed toward third, feeling the *thump-thump-thump* of my heart pounding in my chest.

Out of the corner of my eye, I sensed movement on the field. Flashes of red Cardinal jerseys zigzagged around me. I ignored them and kept my sights on my coach, like every good base runner should.

Alana must have creamed the ball, I thought.

I didn't look into the stands to see if my parents were watching. I didn't sneak a peek into left field to see if the ball was close. I just kept my eyes glued on Coach Kim. After another second, she threw her arms down to the ground—the signal to slide!

The ball must be heading toward third! I needed to hit the dirt and get my feet there first.

Just like in practice, I lifted my left leg while straightening my right, throwing them into a figure-four position as I dropped to the ground and threw my hands in the air. The momentum pushed my straight body across the sandy gravel toward third base. My foot hit the base a split second before I heard the familiar *thwack* of ball hitting glove.

"Safe!" called the umpire.

Before taking my foot off the base, I made a *T* with my hands. The umpire called, "Time-out!"

"Excellent base running, Rana!" Coach Kim said, giving me a pat on the back.

I straightened up and wiped the dust out of my eyes. I felt my back pocket to make sure my batting glove hadn't slipped out since I took it off at first base. Some girls would then wipe the dirt and gravel from their pants. But I liked to keep it. It reminded me that the game wasn't over yet.

Just as I had suspected, Alana had made it safely to second. I flashed her a thumbs-up.

Despite her small frame, Alana was one of the best hitters on our team. She had the upper body strength to bring the bat around quickly and the patience to know when to hold back. The same smarts that helped her on the ice hockey rink also worked well in the batter's box.

I loved watching Alana at the plate. And secretly, I wished that I could hit like her.

"OK," Coach Kim whispered into my ear, "one more run and this thing is ours. Remember, be smart. Take your lead, but don't get trapped in a pickle. They're probably expecting the sacrifice fly, so make sure you get back here as soon as the ball goes into the air and tag up. Got it?"

I nodded yes in reply. *I got this*, I thought.

Tempted to peek into the energetic bleachers behind me, I focused instead on Martina, the Cardinals pitcher on the mound. Martina was tall. Easily the tallest in our entire eighth grade at Cape Elementary.

When we played softball in PE during the school year, I liked being on Martina's team. As a catcher, I appreciate a strong pitcher who can throw more than just fastballs. But this wasn't a PE scrimmage. It was the Cape Summer League season ender, and we were opponents.

Martina's dark, curly hair poked out from every end of her cap, sticking to her forehead in sweaty globs. She knew I could steal and kept throwing side glances my way in an attempt to scare me back to base.

Not going to happen, I thought.

Lara was up next, batting cleanup, the fourth and most important spot in the lineup. Lara is our star third baseman. Nothing gets by her glove.

She is also an expert at hitting the sacrifice fly—a hit so far into the outfield that it gives the base runner a chance to tag up and get to the next base before the outfielder can throw it back.

Lara kept one foot out of the batter's box. She took practice swings as she turned to Coach Kim for the signal.

Coach Kim tugged on her right ear—the signal for take a pitch. Then she touched her nose and patted her head. Those were just meaningless signals meant to confuse the other team. Finally, she clapped her hands and stomped her feet—the signal for no more signals.

I love signals. It's like a secret coded language that only our team knows. When I'm catching behind the plate, I use signals to communicate with the pitcher and tell her which types of pitches to throw. Like Coach Kim, I mix in some silly signs that mean absolutely nothing at all in the hopes of throwing the batter off her game.

Lara nodded her head and stepped her other foot into the box. Martina placed the ball in her glove and gave me another look.

My feet itched to get off the base and creep toward home plate. Lara was not going to swing at this first pitch. But that didn't mean I couldn't try to fake out the Cardinals. I was ready to run as soon as that ball left Martina's hand.

Martina gave me the side-eye.

Then she cradled the ball in her glove and took a step backward with her right foot. As her foot moved behind her, her arm swung up and back, then launched into the air over her head. Her arm circled back around her body and brushed by her hip bone. She released the ball, fingers stretched out toward home plate in the perfect follow-through.

Lara stood there and did nothing, taking the pitch as directed. The ball hit firmly into the center of the catcher's mitt.

"Strike one!" called the umpire.

I hustled back to the base, keeping my foot on the bag until Martina walked back to the mound. Coach Kim swiped her forehead—the signal for sacrifice fly. Lara stepped back into the batter's box, ready for the second pitch.

Remember, be smart, I thought. *If you're caught off the base, she can throw you out.*

Martina moved quickly and set up for her next pitch, trying to throw Lara off rhythm. Lara started her backswing before I could take much of a lead. This time, Lara swung hard and connected. The ball bounced off the bat, hurtling up into the sky toward center field in a giant arc. It was a perfect sacrifice fly!

I sprinted back to third and set my foot on the base, tagging up. When the Cardinals center fielder caught the ball, I could sprint toward home plate and try to beat the throw.

The center fielder shielded her eyes from the sun with her glove as she tracked the ball in the sky. As the white orb fell back toward Earth, she took a few steps forward, building up her throwing momentum. I dug my heel into the base, getting ready to run like my life depended on it.

As soon as the ball smacked against her glove, I took off toward home. She had a strong arm, as all center fielders should. But I knew I could beat her. I pumped my arms and connected with the energy pulsing through my legs.

The field erupted in excitement. Fans cheered for both sides. Teammates in the dugouts jumped up and down.

The Cardinals' catcher planted herself squarely over home plate, ready to block my slide. Her glove was open and ready. This was going to be close.

Even if the ball made it home, I could still knock it out of the catcher's mitt and the run would count. *Thump!* I hit the dirt with as much energy as I could muster. My body collided with the catcher and everything went suddenly quiet.

As the dust settled around me, I looked up at the umpire.

"Safe!" he yelled. "Dodgers win!"

My teammates poured out of the dugout, piling on top of me before I had a chance to stand up. Parents, friends, and fans cheered madly from the sidelines, waving blue-and-yellow pom-poms and blowing noisemakers.

"Last to first! Last to first!" they cheered.

"Last to first" had been our motto all season, after finishing last year in a disappointing last place. After making some changes to our roster and refocusing on the fundamentals, we knew this season could be ours. And now it was!

Somehow, I dug my way out from under the victory pile. Amidst the chaos, I saw Maya push her way through the crowd. She had a pencil tucked into her curly hair and her blue journal in hand.

"Rana," Maya shouted through the noise, "can I get a comment for the newspaper? You just scored the winning run to clinch the first place spot for the Dodgers! What are you going to do next?"

I smiled, basking in the glory of this moment. I couldn't resist. "We're going to Disney World!" I shouted.

TWO

Pizza & Planning

"Quit hogging the pepperoni, Louie!" Alana complained.

We were sitting around a table in the back room of Pete's, the best pizza restaurant on the Cape. Normally, during the crowded summer months when the population of our tiny fishing town rose from 15,000 to 115,000, it was impossible to get a table. Some people even waited two hours! But not us year-round locals. We just got takeout and called it a day.

My neighbors grumbled when the summer season hit. They complained about tourists clogging up our streets and dirtying the beaches.

But I didn't mind when things got crowded in the summer. It felt exciting, like the world was finally paying attention to our little spot on the coast.

Besides, summer tourists were a huge part of my dad's business. He was the harbor master. During summer weekends, he offered cruises along the coastline. He told visitors old fishing tales and ghost stories as they floated past elegant waterfront estates.

But today was a special day. Summer League softball was huge on the Cape. Since the girls in the league needed to live here year-round to play, it was especially important for locals like Pete, who reserved this room every year for the season champs.

I bit into another deliciously greasy slice of cheese pizza and looked around at our celebrating teammates, coaches, and families. I was especially glad that, this year, the winning team was us.

Some of the team parents had surprised us by sneaking over early and decorating the room in

Dodger blue and yellow. Pictures of each girl on the team hung from a sparkly banner across the center of the room.

"Relax," Louie said, pushing the pan of pepperoni across the table toward Alana, "there's plenty left for all of us. How many pieces have you had so far, anyway?" she asked.

"Noneya," Alana answered through a mouthful of pepperoni.

"Huh?" asked Louie.

"Noneya business!" Alana answered. She clapped her hands together and threw her head back with laughter. "Oh boy!" she said. "I just crack myself up sometimes."

Louie looked at me and we both laughed. Louie, Alana, Maya, and I had been best friends since kindergarten. Even after all that time together, we weren't sick of Alana's corny jokes.

Maya plopped down in the chair next to me and placed her journal and pencil down on the table. Then she reached for a slice of sausage pizza and let out a happy sigh.

"I'm getting some really great quotes for my article," she said. "I think the Dodgers might be my favorite team to cover!"

"Hey, watch it," said Louie. "You covered my dance troupe this spring, don't you remember?"

Maya smiled. "How could I forget? My neck is still sore from trying to follow all those tumbling routines," she said.

Maya was a junior sports reporter for the *Cape Chronicle*, our local newspaper. She covered any sporting event imaginable, including Cape Elementary, Cape High, and Summer League softball. On top of that, Maya was also the only girl sports broadcaster in town!

"So," she said, reaching for another slice, "what's next for the Dodgers?"

"Playoffs are next weekend," I answered. "The top four teams play each other in a tournament for the whole shebang. Since we just clinched first, we get to play the fourth-place team, the Astros."

"So that means the Cardinals will play the Giants?" Maya asked.

"You've certainly done your research!" said Louie.

Maya shrugged her shoulders. "Any good sports reporter knows her facts," she said.

"Great base running, Rana," came a voice from over my shoulder.

I turned around to see Lara standing over me. The oldest girl in our grade, Lara was almost a year older than us and already about to turn fourteen. I never felt comfortable around her for some reason, even though we had been teammates for two years now.

The rest of our infield stood next to her. Dottie, our team captain and star pitcher, and Nicole, our shortstop. Karla, our first baseman, and Maisy, our second baseman, were the youngest girls on the team. They had each played travel leagues since grade school and were the first seventh graders to ever make the competitive Cape Summer League.

"Thanks, Lara," I answered. "It was a team effort, though. You hit a great game. Four for four! That sac-fly at the end was clutch. How do your arms feel?"

"Never better," Lara answered. "I'll ice them tonight, but I should be good to go for batting practice tomorrow."

Dottie smiled at me.

"Great catching, Rana," she said. "Sorry about that wild pitch in the third. I don't know how you kept it in front of you. I really could have cost us another run."

"The star pitcher and her dependable catcher," Maya murmured to herself. "That could be a good story angle."

"Are you still taking batting lessons?" Lara asked me.

It wasn't much, but I sensed a change in her tone. She stood up a little straighter and adjusted her jersey.

"Me? Oh, yeah," I answered a bit sheepishly. "You know, just for fun."

"Well, as long as it's just for fun. I was starting to think you wanted my spot in the lineup," Lara said, forcing a casual tone.

She patted my shoulder, a little harder than necessary, and walked away.

"Why do you let her do that?" Alana asked.

"Do what?" I said.

"Let her bully you into thinking you can't hit," Louie jumped in. "Your work with Coach Kim is paying off. Remember that line drive you hit last week? You've definitely had fewer strikeouts this year. You even made it on base today!"

"Yeah," I agreed, "but that was from a walk."

"Whatever," answered Louie. "That just proves you have a good eye. It still helped the team!"

I'd wanted to be a strong batter for as long as I could remember. I was pretty good at reading the situation and calling pitches, thanks to all of my years behind the plate. But my batting skills weren't that great. I tended to strike out a lot.

The rules of the game said that I had to hit, but I could tell the rest of the team didn't expect much when I was in the batter's box. Coach Kim was the first coach who'd seen potential and taken the time to give me extra batting practice.

"Don't worry about it." I brushed it off. "I appreciate you sticking up for me, but I'm fine. Really. Let's celebrate!"

Louie, Maya, and Alana exchanged a look.

"So," said Maya, changing the subject, "let's go over the playoff schedule again. I want to be sure I have it right in my article. First round is Friday night. Then, the two teams that win on Friday get to play in the championship on Saturday, right?"

"Yep," said Alana.

"Consider yourself fact-checked," added Louie.

Maya laughed and jotted some notes in her journal. "It's pretty exciting," she said, "but don't forget the real highlight of next weekend—my birthday!"

"Oh, right!" I said. "I'm sorry. We've been so focused on the playoffs that we haven't talked about your birthday at all! It's a big one. Thirteen! Can you believe you're going to be a teenager?"

Maya was the first in our group to reach her teenage years. We'd been talking about this all year long. How could we almost forget now that it was so close?

"Don't worry!" said Maya. "I've been so busy these past few weeks that I haven't had much time to plan anything. I think we're just going to have a small barbeque at the house on Monday, after playoff weekend is over. Cici said she'd bake a cake. Can you girls come?"

"Of course!" said Louie.

"Your sister is baking a cake? Count me in!" said Alana.

"Wouldn't miss it for the world," I added.

"Great!" said Maya. "Now, I've got to run."

She stood up, grabbed her journal, and pushed in her chair.

"I need to get this article to Mac by 5:00 p.m. if it's going to make tomorrow's paper. Great game, girls!" she said.

As Maya walked away, Alana reached for another slice of pizza. "I feel kind of bad for Maya," she said, wiping a glob of sauce from her chin. "Shouldn't she be doing something a bit more exciting for her thirteenth birthday?"

"Yeah," agreed Louie. "You only turn thirteen once, right?"

Just then, an idea popped into my head. I smiled.

"Uh-oh," said Louie. "I know that look. You've got an idea, don't you?"

"No, Rana," groaned Alana. "I can't handle another one of your ideas. Remember when you convinced me to try skating on your homemade stilts?"

Before I had a chance to defend myself, I was sneak-attacked from behind by Darius and Jasper, my two younger brothers.

"Argh, guys, get off!"

"Me too! Me too," said Ruby, my baby sister.

She jumped on my lap and squeezed her chubby arms around me. Her brown

27

curly hair stuck out in two tiny pigtails from the top of her head. Her eyes were dark and deep unlike mine, which were bright blue.

Between Mom's darker Persian features and Dad's Irish heritage, we were an interesting mix. But if you looked closely, you could see that all four kids had the same nose, Mom's, and the same long eyelashes, Dad's.

"Rana Parisi," laughed Alana as she watched me struggle, "softball star and babysitter extraordinaire!"

"Come on you hooligans," said Mom. She walked over to the table. With one hand, she lifted Ruby from my lap, and with the other, she nudged Jasper and Darius off to the side.

"Time to get going. Ready, Rana?" she asked.

"Yep," I answered.

The pizza party had been fun, but I was ready to get home and start focusing on the playoffs. Maybe I'd sneak in some batting practice with Dad before bed, too. I pushed in my chair and leaned down close to Louie and Alana.

"I do have an idea," I whispered, "but it's a secret. Come to my house after practice tomorrow and I'll explain."

The girls rolled their eyes and exchanged a look. Before they could ask any questions, I grabbed my glove and hurried out the door.

THREE

Batting & Practice

"Nice hit!" Coach Kim said.

She reached into the bucket of balls and tossed another into her glove.

Like always, I met Coach Kim about an hour before regular practice. We'd been working on my batting.

Coach Kim was awesome. She was young, somewhere in her midtwenties. As a student at Cape High, she made the National High School All-Star Softball Team every year. Now, she coached Summer League softball on the Cape and goes south in the winter to be the assistant coach for her old college team.

Coach Kim was also the first coach who'd ever really taken the time to help me with my batting form. She believed that, since I was a good catcher, I could also be a good hitter.

Behind the plate, it was my job to help the pitcher figure out what to throw next. Two balls, no strikes? Time for a fastball. Batter's been swinging early? Throw a changeup.

As a catcher, I could anticipate what a pitcher was going to throw. If I could just get my form right, I could be dangerous at the plate.

Until now, I had spent every warm weekend practicing with Dad in the backyard. His tips had been helpful, and I was getting better. But it was time for a professional to step in. When Coach Kim offered private lessons, I jumped at the chance.

"Again," she shouted, getting ready to throw another pitch. "Remember, don't worry about power, just focus on form."

I closed my eyes and visualized the fundamentals. Grip. Hand position. Swing. Contact. Follow-through.

Grip. I stacked my hands right over left and gripped the bat, applying pressure with my fingertips, but keeping my wrists loose. I choked up slightly, inching my hands a little farther up the handle.

Hand position. I extended my hands out in front of my chest about three or four inches. I made sure to keep the bat centered between my shoulders, elbow down and relaxed. I moved my hands and elbows back and forth just a little bit, like Coach Kim showed me. This was called the power position, or power alley.

Swing. As the ball came toward me, I started the swing in my legs and hips. I pushed off the ball of my back foot, rotating my hips while keeping them parallel to one another. I made sure my head and eyes stayed level and still, something I used to forget, which would cause me to lose sight of the ball.

I kept my front elbow at ninety degrees and brought the nob of the bat toward the ball. Then, I rotated my wrists to bring the rest of the bat around. I drove my shoulders toward the ball, which kept my hands up and my hips open.

Contact. This pitch was right down the middle. I aimed to make contact directly opposite my front hip. When the ball connected with my bat, I

kept my arms level and swung through. I extended fully, looking down both arms and the barrel of the bat. I shifted most of my body weight to the front foot, but I remembered to stay balanced.

Follow-through. The swing didn't end once you made contact. I rolled my wrists over completely and swung all the way through. I finished with my hands near my front shoulder as the ball shot down the third base line.

"Line drive!" Coach Kim yelled. She dropped her glove and ran toward me. "Wow, Rana," she said. "I'd hate to be playing third with a hit like that! You could have taken the legs right out from underneath someone!"

She tugged the brim of my helmet down over my eyes and we both laughed. A car door slammed in the distance. The rest of the team would be here any second for regular practice.

"Thanks, Coach Kim," I said with a smile. "I owe it all to you."

"Oh, no you don't," Coach Kim replied. "You've put a lot of work into this, kiddo. Don't sell yourself short. Just keep practicing your form and you'll be a threat at the plate in no time."

As we walked toward the dugout, Louie and Alana arrived, followed by Lara and the rest of the team. Coach Lucy, our assistant coach, asked some of the girls to help her carry the bags of bats, helmets, and catcher's equipment to the dugout.

Alana dropped an extra-large bag of sunflower seeds on the bench. Louie spat a mouthful of slimy shells into the dirt.

"Such a lady," I joked.

"OK, we're dying to know," Alana said. "What is this top secret idea of yours?"

"Yeah," said Louie, "please tell me it's not like the time you thought throwing stink bombs in the visitors' dugout would be a fun prank."

I smirked, remembering that particularly fun afternoon.

"I'll tell you after practice," I answered slyly. "You can sleep over tonight, right?"

"Right," they answered.

"Excellent," I said, reaching for my mitt. "Then we'll have all night to talk about it."

"Nice hit," Lara said under her breath as she walked by. "Just remember, I'm batting cleanup."

"Easy, tiger," said Alana. "We're all on the same team here."

"All right girls," Coach Kim yelled, "hustle home."

We all knew what that meant. Base running drills would be first. We assembled into a straight line behind home plate and waited for Coach Kim's instructions.

"Great game yesterday," she said. "I know I said it already, but I'm so proud of what we've accomplished this year. No matter what happens in the playoffs, nobody can ever take this season away from us."

"Last to first!" Louie shouted.

"Exactly," Coach Kim said. "But now we've got to stay focused. The Astros are no easy team to beat, and we can't take them for granted. Let's warm up with some base running. On my whistle!"

We did this drill at every practice, so no further explanations were needed. At the sound of the whistle, each runner took a turn sprinting to first base as fast as she could before heading to the back of the line. Three more rounds followed, with sprints to second, third, and home plate. By the end, we had all broken a good sweat.

Next, Coach Kim organized us into three groups for rotating drills.

"Louie," Coach Kim said, handing her a bat, "take this group to the outfield and shag flies. Mix it up and keep them on their toes! Start deep. It's easier to run toward the ball than to backpedal."

Louie was great at tracking fly balls and started every game in right field.

"Alana," she said, "head to the fence with this group and practice swings. The fence is eye level, so if you hit the ball over it, you need to adjust your form. The ball should hit the fence squarely in front of you. Lead with your elbow, and pull the bat around. No pop-ups unless we're hitting the sacrifice fly."

She turned to Coach Lucy for the third and final group. "Coach Lucy will work on laying down the bunt," she said.

"You two," Coach Kim added, pointing to Dottie and me, "let's get those arms warmed up."

The hot August sun blazed down as we moved through the drills. After each rotation, Coach Kim called for a break. As we sat on the grass, guzzling cold water, she reviewed signals.

We finished practice with another baserunning drill. By the end, I was completely soaked in sweat.

"Great work, girls," Coach Kim said as we packed up our gear. "Drink lots of water and get some rest tonight. I'll see you in the morning. Only three practices left until playoffs!"

As we walked off the field, I noticed Maya riding her bike straight toward us. She must have been watching our practice and taking notes for her articles.

"Don't tell Maya about the sleepover," I whispered quickly.

The girls looked confused.

"Why not?" asked Louie.

"Just trust me," I urged.

Maya got closer.

"Looking good out there!" she said.

"Did you also go to the Astros practice?" asked Alana. "Can you tell us what they're working on?"

"Wouldn't you like to know!" Maya pulled her finger across her closed mouth in the my-lips-are-sealed motion. "What are you up to now?" she asked.

Alana and Louie looked at me and said nothing.

"My mom's going to give these two a lift home and then I think I might rest a bit. Need to reserve my energy, you know?" I said casually, hoping I could avoid her reporter's curiosity.

"Oh, OK," Maya answered. "Well, I need to get going myself. The Cardinals are practicing on the upper fields, and I'd like to get some notes on their team, too. I'm writing a pre-playoff article and Mac needs it by 8:00 tonight. See you later!"

Maya waved and peddled up the hill toward the distant upper fields. When she was out of earshot, Louie and Alana pounced.

"What was that all about?" Alana asked. "Why couldn't we tell Maya the truth?"

"Because," I answered, "the truth is that we're going to throw her a surprise thirteenth birthday bash, and we need to start planning immediately!"

FOUR

Keeping Secrets

"First things first. We need to pick a theme!"

Louie, Alana, and I were sprawled out across my bedroom floor, flipping through magazines. I was right—they had loved the idea instantly and couldn't wait to start brainstorming party plans.

We decided to have the party on Sunday, the day after the championship game, since most of our friends would be around for the playoffs. That was less than a week away, so we had to act fast!

"Pretty flowers!" Ruby giggled, pointing to a page in my magazine.

Mom had asked if we could watch Ruby for a bit while she read with Darius and Jasper downstairs. Mom was an English teacher at Cape Elementary, so it was fun having the summers off together.

The only problem was, as a teacher, she gave us summer homework like reading or working on math problems. All of the other kids got to take a three-month break!

"Be careful, Ruby," I said, gently pulling the magazine out of her chubby fingers. "We don't want to rip the pretty picture."

"What about a futuristic theme?" Alana asked excitedly. "I'm sure I could build some sort of simple robot that could serve food or maybe even greet the guests!"

Alana loved her STEAM projects and spent any free periods she had at school in the science lab or MakerSpace tinkering on her latest inventions.

"Not that I don't love it," Louie answered, "but I don't love it."

Alana rolled her eyes and flipped the page.

"What about a garden tea party?" I suggested.

"Barf!" Louie complained. "That's way too girly, Rana. Don't even think about asking me to wear a dress to this thing."

I laughed. How I could I have thought Louie would go for something like that?

Ruby waddled over to my bookshelf and pulled a few books onto the ground. She flipped through the pages, clapping her hands together as she looked at the bright illustrations.

"Story, Rana! Story!" she said.

"Not now, Ruby," I said. "We're busy. Maybe later?"

This was not what Ruby wanted to hear. She puffed out her bottom lip. Ugh, how could I resist that face?

"OK," I reluctantly agreed. "Bring me a book."

Ruby smiled and waddled over to me, book in hand. I looked at the cover.

"*Summertime Picnic*," I read.

Just then, another lightbulb went off in my brain.

"Ruby!" I said. "You're a genius!"

"Huh?" asked Louie and Alana.

"Summertime picnic!" I said, "I think we just found our party theme!"

In perfect timing, Mom pushed open the bedroom door with a tray of chocolate chip cookies and glasses of cold lemonade.

"For the helpful babysitters," she offered.

"Yum! Thanks, Mrs. P!" Alana said.

She pushed some magazines off of the bedside table and made a space for the tray. We each took two cookies and a glass of lemonade.

"Come on, little one," Mom said to Ruby. "Time for your afternoon nap." Ruby crawled into Mom's arms and they left the room.

"So, summertime picnic?" said Louie, chewing thoughtfully. "I think I could get into that."

"We could have it on the picnic tables down by Lambert's Beach," I suggested. "It's free to the public and right on the water, so we could go swimming or play beach games, too!"

"I love it!" said Alana as she reached for her third cookie. "Think we can pull it off?"

We spent the rest of the afternoon organizing the party plans. I kept notes as we delegated the details.

I was in charge of decorations. There would be red and white checkered tablecloths and bunches of red, white, and blue balloons. We'd have small arrangements of hydrangeas, Maya's favorite, and, of course, number thirteen-themed party plates, napkins, and banners.

Alana took on the menu. She called our favorite restaurant, the Clam Strip. It's just a shanty beach hut. But it has the best seafood in town. She ordered platters of lobster rolls, tubs of clam chowder, and buckets of their famous salty-dog fries.

Louie's family owned Lin Lane, the only general store in town, which carried a large supply of portable beach games. She called her dad, who happily agreed to let us use a beanbag game, a beach volleyball set, horseshoes, and boogie boards!

"I think that covers everything!" I said, snapping my notebook shut.

"Wait," said Louie, "we forgot one very important thing."

"What?" I asked.

"The guests!" she said. "How are we going to invite people without Maya finding out? You know how terrible our class is at keeping secrets."

"Hmm, good point," I said. "Why don't we wait and invite everyone on Friday afternoon after our playoff game? Most of our friends will be there, and this way they only need to keep the secret for forty-eight hours."

"Should we tell Maya's parents?" Alana asked.

I thought for a minute.

"Nah," I finally answered. "Too risky. Let's just keep it between us."

"Girls! Dinner's ready!" Mom called from downstairs.

"Yay!" Alana jumped to her feet. "I'm starving! Let's eat."

As we finished a dinner of Mom's famous spaghetti and meatballs, I suggested we ride our bikes into town to get ice cream at the Scoop.

"What if Maya's there?" asked Louie nervously. "She could see us all together. That would really hurt her feelings."

"What are the odds?" I asked, grabbing my helmet from the hook near the back door. "Besides, she's busy writing her article, remember? She said it was due by 8:00 p.m., and it's only 7:30 now, so she's probably still working. We'll be fine! Alana, is your brother Timmy behind the counter tonight?"

"Yep," answered Alana.

She swiped a crusty piece of bread around her plate, soaking up every last drip of the juicy spaghetti sauce.

"Hey!" Alana said. "We can ask him to bring the Scoop ice cream truck to Maya's party!"

"Great idea!" I said. "See girls? This is official party-planning business now, so we have to go."

Louie reluctantly agreed and followed us to the driveway. After a short bike ride, we rolled up to the popular ice cream spot.

"Sheesh!" Alana rolled her eyes. "The line is all the way out the door! Tourists," she mumbled.

We took our spot at the end of the line and started debating which flavors to get. Just as we were about to reach the front, I felt a tiny tap on my shoulder.

"What are you guys all doing here?"

I turned around to see Maya staring at us. She was frowning.

Oh no! I thought.

Louie and Alana looked panicked. I gave them a look that meant, *just keep cool.*

"Maya! There you are," I said quickly. "We were hoping you'd be here."

"What?" Maya asked, a confused look on her face.

"We tried calling your house, but nobody picked up," I lied. "We decided last minute to get some ice cream and wanted you to come, too. We're so glad you're here!"

"Yeah," Alana added, catching on. "When nobody picked up, we figured you were still busy working on your article."

"That's weird," she said. "I don't remember hearing our phone ring."

She looked at us suspiciously. The tension was killing me.

"Oh well," she said, her face relaxing a bit. "Let me just go tell my parents I'm going to stand in line with you guys. That's OK, right?"

"Of course!" I said, maybe a little too loudly. "We'll wait for you."

As Maya ran to the end of the line, Louie jabbed my shoulder.

"See?" she said. "I knew that would happen."

"Relax!" I said, brushing it off. "I think she bought it. We've got nothing to worry about. Now, mint chip or cookie dough?"

FIVE

Secrets & Lies

"One out. Runners on first and third. What are our options?" Coach Kim shouted from the plate.

It was later in the week, at the end of our final practice before Friday's playoff game. We were working on fielding situations. I crouched behind home, visualizing the potential plays. Dottie stood on third base, Alana at first. Depending on how they ran the bases, there were a few options.

"Check home, throw second," Lara yelled back.

Even though she wasn't forced to run, there was a chance Dottie would try to make it home. So we had to check that first. If she ran, I would be waiting for the throw. If not, Nicole would be at second for the force out throw that would get Alana.

I kept visualizing. Coach Kim would want everyone to know exactly what they would do if the ball came to them.

"What else?" Coach Kim asked.

If the hit was a strong line drive to right, we could turn a double play and end the inning. Even if Dottie made it home, the run wouldn't count.

"Check third, throw the double play," Maisy yelled from her spot between first and second base. "If Dottie hesitates, I throw to Nicole at second to get the lead runner. Then, she throws back to Karla at first."

"Right," Coach Kim answered. "Anything else?"

I knew a third option, but before I could call it out, Louie waved her hands in right field. She had the strongest arm on the team, thanks to all of her dance troupe's handstands and tumbling. She could easily reach home plate with a single throw.

"Sacrifice fly!" Louie yelled. "Anticipate the tag up and throw home."

"Excellent," Coach Kim responded. "If that's the case, Rana, make sure you protect the plate. She'll run straight into you to try and knock the ball loose. So get low and stay balanced."

"Got it," I answered, bringing the catcher's mask down over my face.

Coach Kim lifted the bat.

"Ready position!" she yelled.

Everyone in the field crouched into their stance. Alana and Dottie took their leads off the base. I visualized each option one final time, not knowing which would come, but prepared for any.

Coach Kim tossed the ball in the air and smacked it hard down the center of the field.

I popped up, opening my glove ready for a throw that might come my way.

Nicole sprinted over to second as Maisy charged the ball. She kept her glove to the dirt and scooped up the ball near the pitcher's mound. Before making the throw, she quickly checked third to assess the situation. Dottie had stopped halfway down the baseline, hesitating just enough so that she forced the double play.

Maisy turned on a dime and threw the ball to second, where Nicole already had one foot on the bag. With the attention off of her, Dottie ran for home. I crouched low and opened my mitt.

Nicole caught the ball right before Alana slid into the base, then turned and threw to first. The ball smacked against the inside of Karla's glove, beating Coach Kim to the base.

Dottie slid into home, trying to knock me off of my feet, but I jumped out of the way in time.

"You're out!" Coach Lucy yelled from the dugout. "Great double play, girls!"

I pulled the catcher's mitt off and offered Dottie a hand. "Sorry, Charlie," I said. "Your run doesn't count."

She laughed as she wiped the dirt from her legs.

"I so would have been safe," she said.

"Bring it in, girls!" Coach Kim called. She jogged to the pitcher's mound and we formed a large circle around her.

I guzzled the rest of my water and let the surprisingly cool breeze wash over my sweaty face. I loved the late afternoon practices we had at the end of summer. The sky had turned from bright turquoise to a pale periwinkle, and the salty breeze from the nearby ocean began making its way inland.

"Excellent work today," Coach Kim began. "We've done everything we can to prepare for the Astros. I'm proud of all the hard work you girls have put in. We're the strongest we've ever been. As long as we stick to our game plan and play smart tomorrow, the Astros don't stand a chance! Huddle up!"

We gathered on the mound, throwing our hands into the center for a final cheer.

"Go Dodgers!" we yelled.

As we walked back to the dugout, Lara sidled up next to me.

"Sticking with our usual game plan," she said under her breath. "Don't worry, I'll kill the ball. Maybe I'll even hit a home run. That should make it exciting for you to run the bases."

"If you keep talking like that, Lara, I'm going to have to tell Coach," Dottie said, coming to my rescue.

"Whatever," Lara grumbled and walked away.

Dottie patted me on the back. I kept my face down, not wanting her to see my cheeks red with embarrassment.

"Don't listen to her," she said. "She's just nervous about losing her spot in the lineup. We saw you hitting with Coach Kim before practice. You were making good contact! Besides, running is just as important. Lara's just jealous that you're a smarter runner."

I felt my cheeks return to normal.

"Thanks, Dottie," I said. "See you tomorrow."

Alana and Louie met me in the dugout. Our parents had agreed to let us walk down to the Clam Strip for dinner after practice. The restaurant was less than a mile from the fields.

Since it was only five thirty, the sun wasn't setting anytime soon. But we only had an hour. We needed to get to bed early for the big game tomorrow. Maya was meeting us there, giving us time to review final party plans on our walk.

"Wait until you see the paper plates and napkins I found," I said as we made our way to the restaurant. "They are red and white checkered with a glittery number 13 in the center. Perfect for a summer picnic soirée!"

Alana and Louie walked on either side of me.

"Soirée? Aren't we fancy?" Louie joked. "I have all the party games in my garage. Dad even threw in extras so we can have a few games going."

"That reminds me," said Alana, "I have good news! Timmy said the Scoop will let him bring over the ice cream truck for an hour. They're even letting us have the cones for free as a treat for making the playoffs!"

I smiled. Everything was coming together perfectly! Now, all we had to do was invite our friends after the game tomorrow and keep it a secret from Maya just a little bit longer.

The faded gray shingled walls of the Clam Strip came into view. A line of people snaked out from the takeout window as families happily took cartons of freshly fried food over to nearby Lambert's Beach.

Maya sat at a picnic table near the water.

"Great table!" I said. "How did you manage to get it with this crowd?"

Maya seemed to have forgotten about the incident at the Scoop. Unfortunately, though, she had called my house one night this week when Louie and Alana were over working on the invitations.

I had tried my best to keep the girls quiet. But Maya had heard the background noise and asked what was going on. I had made up some lame story about Darius and Jasper staying up past their bedtime, but I could tell Maya was suspicious.

As we approached her table, I felt nervous butterflies rising in my stomach. Thankfully, Maya had a huge smile on her face. She scooted over and gestured for me to sit across from her.

"I came early to organize my notes because guess what!" she said excitedly. "I just found out I'll be broadcasting the playoff games tomorrow, and the championship the day after that!"

"Wow!" said Alana. "Congratulations. Will it be on Cape Radio, too?"

"Yep!" Maya answered proudly.

Louie dropped her glove in the sand and plopped down on the bench.

"Well," she said, "let me make it easier for you. I don't know about the first game, but the second is going to end with a win for the Dodgers! Astros are going down!"

We laughed and ordered heaping plates of chicken legs and mashed potatoes. The greasy goodness raised our spirits even higher as we ate and talked. For the first time all week, I felt relaxed.

"Are you excited for your birthday, Maya?" Alana asked as she swiped the final chicken leg from Maya's plate.

Maya shrugged her shoulders. Her jovial spirit faded a bit.

"Yeah, I guess," she answered. "I haven't been able to plan much, to tell you the truth. We're just having a simple barbeque. Mom, Dad, Santi, Cici, you guys. Maybe a couple of other people. Nothing fancy, but hopefully it will be fun."

"Oh, I have a feeling it will be fun," Louie said.

I kicked Louie under the table.

"Ow!" she said. "Why'd you kick me?"

Maya gave us a confused look.

"Sorry," I said, trying to keep a straight face. "Leg cramp."

Alana and Louie stifled nervous giggles under their breath. Maya grinned and quickly excused herself to use the bathroom. When she was out of earshot, I leaned over the table.

"What was that?" I whispered, annoyed. "You're going to give away the surprise! She totally knows something is up now."

"Do you think?" Alana asked. She licked a glob of ketchup from her palm.

"Definitely," I answered. "Did you see her smile and rush to leave the table?"

"Sorry," Louie said sheepishly. "She just looked so bummed about her birthday. We haven't spent

much time with her this week, so I thought I'd say something nice to lift her spirits."

I sighed. We had worked so hard to keep this surprise from Maya. I didn't want to ruin it now.

"Don't worry," I said, softening the edge in my voice. "Here she comes. I'll handle it."

"Uh-oh," said Alana. "I don't like the sound of that."

Maya sat down and stared hard at each of us.

"Why so quiet all of a sudden?" she giggled. "Do you girls know something about my birthday that I don't?"

Louie and Alana looked down at their plates, not saying a word.

I knew what I was about to say would hurt Maya's feelings, but it had to be done.

"Um, about your birthday," I said. "There's a chance I might not be able to go."

Maya's smile fell instantly. "What?" she whispered.

"Turns out, my parents might be taking us to visit our grandparents," I lied. "So I might not be here after all."

"But it's the day after the championship," Maya said. Her voice quivered a bit and her eyes turned glossy with tears. "Your grandparents just visited two weeks ago," she said. "I thought for sure you'd be around. You said you'd be there."

I looked down at my hands, not wanting to see the hurt in her face. "Sorry," I mumbled.

Before anyone could say another word, a horn honked in the distance.

"Our parents are here," Maya whispered.

She grabbed her journal and stood up quickly. I didn't look up as she ran toward her car. After a few moments of silence, Louie cleared her throat.

"Are you sure you needed to do that?" she asked quietly. She and Alana were upset.

I ignored the lump forming in the back of my throat and thought about all the glittery party supplies waiting in my bedroom closet. I forced a cheery smile.

"She'll be fine," I answered, trying to convince myself more than anyone else. "At least she doesn't suspect anything now. Once she sees how hard we worked on the party, she'll forget that even happened."

We tossed our greasy plates into the trash bin and walked silently toward the parking lot. As I hopped into our station wagon, I thought about tomorrow's game and the surprise party. I couldn't tell which I was more nervous for and hoped I hadn't just made a terrible mistake.

SIX

Dodgers vs. Astros

It was the final inning against the Astros. I stood in the batter's box, shaking from head to toe. Both dugouts were empty and the crowd was eerily silent. A shadowy figure stood on the pitcher's mound, staring me down.

The only sound came from the broadcast booth behind home plate. It was Maya's voice.

"In her first at bat of the game," the voice boomed, "Rana Parisi is the Dodgers' only chance for a win. She's already let me down. Let's hope she doesn't fail her team when they need her most."

I turned my head toward the broadcast booth. "I'm sorry!" I whispered, my voice shaky.

The shadowy pitcher started her windup. My knees buckled. Sweat dripped down my forehead, blurring my vision. I tried to focus on my form as the ball made its way toward me, but it was no use. I swung too late, missing completely.

Maya's voice echoed around the field. "Strike three," she yelled. "Dodgers lose."

I woke in a cold sweat. The sky outside my bedroom window was dark blue. Streaks of golden light crept across the horizon. It would be morning soon, but I hadn't slept much thanks to the nightmare that had haunted me all night long.

I checked the clock. It was four o'clock in the morning. Way too early to call Maya.

I hadn't been able to get her hurt expression out of my head and called to apologize when we got home last night. After three unanswered attempts, it was clear Maya was avoiding me. I went to bed early, mumbling that I needed rest.

I made a mental note to find her at the field before our game today. Then, I pulled the covers over my head and tried, in vain, to get some sleep.

After a painfully long morning, a stack of uneaten pancakes, and two more ignored calls to Maya, it was finally time to head to the field.

"Are you sure there's nothing bothering you?" Mom asked.

She and Dad exchanged a concerned glance in the front seat. They had noticed my strange behavior right away and had already asked me three times what was wrong. I pressed my head against the window in the backseat.

"I'm fine," I mumbled for the fourth time. "Just nerves."

"It's OK to be nervous," Dad said, his voice chipper.

Fridays were a busy workday in the summer, especially on a picture-perfect day like today. But he had taken the day off especially for the playoffs, putting someone else in charge of harbor cruises.

"This is a big game!" he continued, trying to raise my spirits. "I'd be worried if you *weren't* nervous! Just try to harness that energy and use it to your advantage. Remember, win or lose, what's most important is that you try your best."

Darius and Jasper poked each other in the ribs as Ruby reached toward me from her car seat. When we reached the parking lot, I quickly said good-bye, grabbed my catcher's equipment from the trunk, and bolted for the field. I needed to find Maya and clear the air.

We were playing on the largest field at the bottom of the hill, reserved for the most special games of the season. With bleachers, stadium lights, a broadcast booth, and a fully stocked snack bar, the field was abuzz with activity.

Spectators climbed down from the bleachers as Cardinals and Giants exited the dugouts. With everything else on my mind, I had completely forgotten they were playing before us.

"Whoa, watch where you're going, Dodger," someone called out.

I looked up to see a group of bright red Cardinal jerseys heading straight toward me.

"Looks like we're on for a rematch," Martina called from the center of the pack. "That is, of course, if you guys don't blow it. Good luck!"

I ignored their smack talk and kept my head down. Alana and Louie appeared at my side as I made my way toward the broadcast booth behind home plate.

"Earth to Rana," Louie said. "Didn't you hear us? We've been calling your name!"

"Sorry," I muttered.

"What did Martina say?" asked Alana. "On second thought, don't tell me. They just crushed the Giants, six to zero. I don't need added pressure."

Louie spat a mouthful of sunflower seed shells into the dirt at our feet. Alana reached into the bag and grabbed a handful for herself.

"I brought the invitations," said Louie. "My mom has them in her purse. We're still going to hand them out after the game, right? A lot of our friends from school are here!"

I didn't answer. I was too distracted by the task at hand.

"What's wrong?" Louie asked. "You don't look so good. Where are you going?"

They stopped at the entrance to the dugout. Most of the other Dodgers had already unloaded their gear. They were with Coach Kim and Coach Lucy on the field for warm-ups.

"Be right back," I said, walking past the dugout toward the broadcast booth.

I spotted Maya through the booth's glass window. She was sitting behind a fancy-looking arrangement of microphones and dials, chatting with a freckle-faced teenager I'd never seen before.

I knocked on the door. Nausea bubbled in my stomach as I tried desperately to think of something to say. Before I could come up with a game plan, the door opened. Maya stared angrily back at me.

"Sorry," she said. "Game's about to start. Booth is closed." With that, she shut the door in my face.

I stood motionless, shock numbing my legs. I knew Maya was upset, but I hadn't expected that.

"Rana!" Coach Kim yelled from the field. "Let's go! Come on!"

I brushed the hot sting of tears from my eyes and jogged over to the team.

Don't fall apart now. Focus, I thought.

"What was that all about?" Alana asked nervously as she tossed me a ball. "Maya looked upset. Is Maya upset?"

"No, no. She's fine," I lied, not wanting to distract her, too. "She just couldn't talk. Had to finish setting up for the broadcast."

"Phew!" Alana answered, a look of relief washing over her face. "You made me nervous for a second."

After a blurry warm-up, the umpire blew her whistle to signal the start of the game. I crouched behind home plate. Then I spotted Mom and Dad sitting in the first row of the bleachers. Darius, Jasper, and Ruby licked happily at melting ice cream cones from the snack bar.

Everyone had family here today. Alana's dad and four older brothers took up the bench behind my family. Louie's parents and grandmother perched on the top row, each holding a pair of binoculars. Maya's older twin siblings, Santi and Cici, chatted with friends near the snack bar.

The remaining bleachers filled up with kids from school and other Summer League teams. There were also lots of unfamiliar tourist faces. An excited hum of energy radiated from the stands as the umpire yelled, "Play ball!"

"Let's go Dodgers!" Mom shouted.

She waved at me and gave a thumbs-up. Maya's voice boomed from the speakers. She sounded joyful and energetic, a far cry from the angry girl who had greeted me before.

"Welcome to our second playoff game of the day, ladies and gentlemen," she announced. "Dodgers vs. Astros. Today's game should be a real nail-biter.

"For our out-of-town guests in need of a recap, the Dodgers just finished the regular season in first place. But the Astros look like they're ready for a rematch. Remember folks, the winner of this game faces the Cardinals in tomorrow night's highly anticipated Cape Summer League season championship, right here under the bright lights. May the best team win!"

I took a deep breath and tried to push nagging worries out of my head.

Will Maya ever speak to me again? Should I just tell her about the surprise party?

I focused on Dottie standing on the pitcher's mound. A tall Astro walked up to the plate, swinging her bat ferociously and stomping her feet. I squatted low and put up my glove.

Dottie stared back at me from the mound. After a few seconds of doing nothing, she stepped off the rubber.

What is she waiting for? I wondered, confused at the delay.

"Rana!" Coach Kim yelled. "Call the pitch!"

Oh, right, I thought. *Get it together.*

I lowered my hand down into the dirt and stuck out one finger, signaling for Dottie to start with a fastball. That would help us get a sense of what this Astro could do.

Dottie nodded and pitched a fast one right down the middle.

"Strike one!" Maya announced from the booth.

At the sound of her voice, I fumbled the ball into the dirt. Quickly, before anyone could notice, I picked it up and tossed it back to Dottie.

This was not going to be easy, I realized.

The rest of the game passed in a dizzying blur. Every time Maya's voice boomed from the broadcast booth, I got distracted and made a silly error. By the end of the final inning, I had struck out twice, overthrown to second, dropped two easy pitches, and even been caught stealing third.

Thankfully, the rest of the team had picked up the slack. Lara's triple late in the game helped us squeak by for a win. The final score was three to two.

Then the teams lined up and shook hands. Coach Kim called us for a postgame huddle back in the dugout.

"Well," Coach Kim started, "that was a little closer than I would have liked. But a win is a win."

I could feel the team sneaking glances my way. The strikeouts were normal, but my other errors were unusual. I avoided eye contact, hoping Coach Kim's speech would end with enough time for me to talk to Maya before she left.

"Let's not dwell on it," Coach Kim continued. "We made it to the championship! Get some rest tonight because you can bet the Cardinals will come out aggressive tomorrow. I'm proud of you girls, but just remember," she paused long enough for me to look up and lock eyes with her, "we have to play smarter tomorrow."

After a quick huddle, I ran out of the dugout. I had to talk to Maya and clear the air. If I couldn't get this apology off of my chest before tomorrow night, I'd be sunk. If I played like I did today, there was a good chance we'd lose the championship.

"Maya?" I banged on the broadcast booth.

The freckle-faced teenager opened the door.

"Sorry," he said. "You just missed her."

SEVEN

Solutions at Sea

Maya's turning thirteen.
We promise, it's not lies!
Let's throw a party and celebrate.
Shh! It's a surprise!

I crumpled up the invitation on my bedside table and tossed it in the wastebasket. I had been so proud when I came up with that cute little rhyme. Now, it made my stomach hurt.

After the game, I came up with an excuse about needing to babysit Ruby, leaving Alana and Louie to hand out the invitations. They had noticed that I was upset. Since they needed to get the invitations out before our friends left, I had escaped before they could ask too many questions.

Now my throat itched and my back hurt. Once again, I hadn't slept a wink. The championship was the furthest thing from my mind. I had tossed and turned all night, debating whether or not to go over to Maya's house and tell her about the party.

We had worked so hard to make it special. I had been holding onto the hope that maybe she would still forgive me. But after seeing how angry she was yesterday, I wasn't so sure.

On the other hand, maybe telling her about the party would make it even worse. She might be upset that I'd spoiled the surprise. I could ruin her thirteenth birthday and our friendship with one wrong move.

I closed my eyes and leaned my throbbing head against the pillow. Before I could debate my dilemma any further, I heard a knock at the door.

"Kiddo?" Dad asked from outside my bedroom. "You awake in there?"

"Yeah," I answered. "Come on in."

Dad poked his head inside the door. He was dressed in casual clothes, holding a bat and a glove.

"There's the star catcher!" he said. "Big day today! Who's up for some batting practice? You never know if they'll need you at the plate."

I smiled despite my terrible mood. Dad was ready in his baseball hat and old gym shoes, but I didn't have the energy to swing a bat right now.

"Maybe in a bit," I answered. "I'm still kind of tired. Didn't sleep great last night."

He walked into the room and sat down at the edge of my bed.

"Worried about the game or something else?" he asked. "Something with Maya, maybe?"

I tugged at the fraying edges of the quilt and avoided his concerned look. I could feel my eyes start to water and my lower lip begin to tremble. I really didn't want to cry.

"How'd you know?" I asked softly.

"Well," he said, "for starters, you've called her like ten times in the past twenty-four hours. Also, there's this."

He handed me a copy of Maya's party invitation.

"How'd you get this?" I asked, shocked.

"Alana and Louie," he answered. "They came by last night looking for you, but you had already gone up to bed. It didn't take much for them to spill the beans. All I had to do was offer Alana some of your mom's apple pie. Honestly, that kid knows how to eat!"

I laughed as Dad wiped away the single tear that had escaped down my cheek.

"Come on," he said. "Let's talk about it on the boat."

Every year, when the summer rush ended, Dad and I went for a Saturday morning sail. He claimed he needed an extra set of hands to check lobster cages or untangle boating lines. But I knew he was really making time for us to spend together, just the two of us. We'd bundle up in hooded sweatshirts, bring a thermos full of hot chocolate, and cruise the shoreline, watching the seagulls peck away at the deserted beach.

During the busy summer months, it was nearly impossible for us to get out on the water together. Today, when everything felt wrong, it sounded like the perfect solution.

"OK," I said. "You make the sandwiches and I'll pack the cooler?"

"You've got yourself a deal," Dad answered. "Meet me downstairs in five."

He turned back before leaving the room.

"Kiddo?" he said. "Don't worry. Everything will be fine."

When we got on the water, the salty air instantly soothed my headache. I closed my eyes, letting the warm breeze wash over my face. It was another picture-perfect day on the Cape. As we cruised along the coast, I admired the brightly colored umbrellas dotting the beaches.

"Start from the beginning," Dad said, handing me a turkey sandwich from the cooler.

I took a bite and let it all out. I told Dad everything. From my idea for the surprise party, to how I tried to throw Maya off by lying to her, to yesterday's incident at the broadcast booth.

As I talked, I could feel a huge weight lift from my shoulders. I wondered why I hadn't asked Dad for his advice earlier.

"Now," I finished, "Maya won't speak to me and I'm pretty sure I'll be a disaster in the game today. So, basically, I've ruined everything."

Dad took the last bite of his sandwich and sipped from his root beer bottle. He hadn't said a word this entire time, just listened carefully as I told him every detail.

"Hmm," he started. "Seems to me like your heart was in the right place, but you forgot to be sensitive of Maya's feelings in the process. You are a good friend, and you were planning something very nice. But, sometimes, we get so caught up in making plans that we forget how our actions make other people feel."

He was right and I knew it. I had wanted so badly to be a good friend to Maya and make her birthday extra special. But at some point, the party plans distracted me from how I was actually treating her. I hadn't been a good friend at all.

To make matters worse, I had dragged Alana and Louie into it. I'd ignored their concerns and asked them to exclude Maya for the sake of the party.

"Also," he continued, "when were you going to tell Maya's parents about this surprise party? Or your mom and me, for that matter? You might be a teenager soon, but you're not getting rid of us that easily. At the very least, you need us to drive!"

I grimaced.

"Oops," I said. "Forgot that small detail. So, should I tell her about the surprise and ruin the party?" Deep down, I already knew the answer.

"Hold on a sec," said Dad. "Just because you ruin the surprise, doesn't mean you'll ruin the party. Even if you tell her, the party can still be a success! The most important thing is that Maya is happy and excited to celebrate with her friends.

"Think about it, kiddo," Dad continued. "If you were about to walk into your party, would you rather be in a good mood or a bad one?"

I pictured the surprised look on Maya's face at the Scoop, the hurt look on her face at the Clam Strip, and the angry look on her face at the broadcast booth.

"Bad mood is an understatement," I said. "Thanks to me, she's probably not excited for her birthday at *all*."

"You won't know unless you try," said Dad. "Can't hit if you don't step up to the plate."

He tossed me a bag of chips. I opened it and shoved a salty handful into my mouth. A silver seagull landed on the boat, squawking hungrily in my direction.

"You're right," I admitted. "But Maya won't even speak to me, and the championship is in three hours. How can I possibly tell her about the party if she won't even look at me?"

Dad winked and pulled a second party invitation from his pocket.

"Well," he said, "you could always invite her."

I reached for the invitation and smiled, knowing exactly who could deliver it.

EIGHT

Untangled Knots

"Here we go, Dodgers, here we go!"

The bleachers on either side of the field buzzed with excitement. Next to our dugout, Dodger fans dressed in blue waved puffy pom-poms in the air. On the other side, a sea of red rooted for the Cardinals.

Every picnic table near the snack bar was taken as happy people gobbled up greasy hot dogs, pizza, and fries. Warm-ups had finished, and the game was about to start.

Alana, Louie, and I huddled behind the bleachers with Ruby. When I got back from the boat ride, I had called and told them everything. I admitted what happened yesterday with Maya and apologized for my behavior, saying that I hadn't been a very good friend to either of them. They came right over, dressed in their uniforms. After a quick group hug, we came up with a plan. Now, it was time to put it into action.

"OK, Ruby," I said, "Maya is inside that gray shed next to Daddy. Go give her the paper!"

"I hope this works," Louie said nervously.

"Well, we only have a few minutes to find out," said Alana. "The coaches are walking onto the field."

I handed Ruby the party invitation.

"Pretty paper," Ruby said, running her finger over the glittery red-and-white checkered edges.

"Don't rip it," I warned as she tugged on the corners. "Daddy has an ice cream for you if you're careful. Look!"

Dad waved at Ruby. He was standing next to the broadcast booth with a vanilla ice cream cone in his hand.

"Sprinkles!" Ruby squealed.

She toddled over toward the booth. When she got there, Dad knocked loudly on the door. For a few seconds, nothing happened. Dad knocked again, louder this time. Finally, the door opened.

Maya looked down, surprised to see Ruby standing in front of her. Ruby dropped the invitation at Maya's feet and scurried behind the booth to Dad and her ice cream reward.

Maya picked up the invitation. When she finished reading it, she looked around, confused.

"That's our cue," I said. "Let's go."

We stepped out from behind the bleachers and walked over to the booth. My stomach was twisted in knots. I worried Maya would slam the door in my face again. But instead, her eyes lit up.

"Guys?" she said, waving the invitation. "What is this?"

"It's the reason why we've been acting so strange lately," I said. "And why I owe you a huge apology."

"You planned a surprise party for me?" she asked, her cheeks blushing red.

"Blame this one," Alana said, patting me on the back.

"Yeah, all her idea," Louie said. "And we all know Rana has the worst ideas," she added with a wink.

Maya smiled weakly.

"I wanted to keep it a surprise," I said. "It's why we've been hanging out without you, so that we could make party plans. It's also why—"

"Why you said you couldn't come to my birthday party?" Maya asked, her smile growing stronger.

I felt the knots in my stomach slowly detangle.

"Yes," I answered. "I was trying to throw you off, but I realize now that I hurt your feelings in the process. I'm sorry. Can you forgive me?"

Without warning, Maya threw her arms around me in a hug, squeezing tightly before letting go.

"Of course!" she answered.

Maya hugged Alana and Louie.

They smiled, too, equally relieved that she accepted our apology.

"This may be the nicest thing anyone's ever done for me," Maya said. "I knew you wouldn't bail on my birthday! I just knew it! A surprise party? How cool!"

"I'm glad you feel that way," said Louie, "because all of our friends are coming."

"We have food and games," added Alana, "even the Scoop's ice cream truck. It'll be a blast!"

At that moment, I didn't care whether the Dodgers won the championship. I had my friend back, and that was all that really mattered.

"Dodgers! Let's go!" Coach Kim shouted from the field.

"Oh, boy," said Maya. "You've got a game to play and I need to get back in the booth. Good luck!"

Alana and Louie ran for the field. Before leaving, I gave Maya one more hug.

"Friends?" I asked.

"Always," she answered. "Now get out there. You've got a championship to win!"

NINE

The Ninth, Again

"Strike three! You're out," the umpire yelled.

It was the bottom of the ninth inning, and Lara had just struck out for the third time.

As expected, the Cardinals had come out swinging. It had been a battle of two strong teams. Aggressive base running. Smart plays. Quick throws.

With my mind off of Maya, I hadn't made any errors behind the plate. But my batting was still off, and I'd only managed to reach first once by getting hit with a pitch.

The game had been tied at three runs apiece. Then the Cardinals hit a triple deep into center field in the top of the eighth, driving in a run and taking the lead. Now, we were down four runs to three. With our final at bat of the game, this was our last chance to win the championship.

Dottie had been up to the plate first. She started a rally by smacking a line drive down the third base line. The energy from the stands rattled Martina and, when she threw a wild pitch over the catcher's head, Dottie easily stole second.

Alana had followed with a shallow fly into left field, getting her to first and Dottie to third.

Normally, this would put us in great position, with no outs and Lara stepping in to bat cleanup. But her bat had been off all game. She popped out in the first, struck out looking in the third, and fell for a changeup in the sixth.

Lara stomped back to the dugout. She dropped her bat against the chain-link fence.

My hands started to sweat. Karla and Maisy were up next in the lineup. We only had one out. If either of them got on base, I would have to bat. My stomach gurgled thinking about the pressure.

"Ugh!" Lara growled.

She sat down next to me on the bench.

"I blew it," she mumbled to herself.

I almost didn't hear her over the cheers that echoed throughout the field. Fans now lined the fences along the first and third base lines, waving homemade signs and singing cheers. I looked over and saw the disappointment in Lara's face.

"No way," I said, trying to lift her spirits. "Your bat got us to this game. Plus, you've played great at third tonight. Nobody thinks you blew it. This is a team effort, remember?"

She wiped at a smear of dirt on her knee.

"Thanks," she said. "Sorry I've been so hard on you. I guess I shouldn't have been so aggressive."

"Don't worry, Lara. Everybody makes mistakes," I said, thinking of how quickly Maya had just forgiven mine. "Plus, with a swing like that, you're allowed to be confident. Maybe, just also be nice?"

"Deal," she laughed.

We turned our attention to the game. Karla stepped into the batter's box. Maisy waited in the on-deck circle.

On the first pitch, Karla hit a line drive down the third base line. The Cardinals shortstop fielded, but held the ball, letting Karla take first and preventing Dottie from running home.

The bases were now loaded.

My heart pounded. Maisy was up. Unless she brought in two runs, we'd still be down by one. I would have to step up to the plate. I wanted to be a strong batter, but not when the championship was on the line!

I grabbed a bat and helmet and nervously stepped into the on-deck circle, selfishly hoping I wouldn't have to hit. I swung the bat feebly a few times, my arms trembling too much to do anything more.

"Let's go Maisy!" I shouted.

It only took three pitches to strike Maisy out. I couldn't believe it.

"Rana!" Coach Kim yelled. "You're up."

My feet froze in place. I couldn't move.

"Rana?" said Coach Kim. "Let's go!"

There was a strong possibility that I was about to throw up.

"Time-out!" called Coach Kim. She ran over to me.

"I know you're nervous, but you can do this," she said. "Just breathe and

remember your form. Don't worry about winning the game, just get on base. That's all we need. I believe in you. We all believe in you, right girls?"

She turned to the dugout. Lara and the rest of the team jumped to their feet.

"Yes!" said Lara.

"You got this!" added Louie.

I gripped my trembling fingers around the bat. Coach Kim returned to her spot next to third base.

My knees wobbled as I headed for home plate. I tried not to look into the field, knowing that Martina was staring me down from the mound. I took a deep breath.

Keep it together, I thought. *You can do this.*

"Now batting for the Dodgers, number thirteen, Rana Parisi!" Maya announced. "Let's show her some love, folks!" Her voice was upbeat and energetic.

The Dodgers bleacher erupted with applause.

"Wahoo! Go Rana!"

Everyone was on their feet and cheering loudly. Ruby, Darius, and Jasper jumped up and down in front of the fence, banging their hands against the metal. Mom waved and Dad made a swinging motion with his arms.

"You got this, kiddo!" he shouted. "Quick hands! Eye on the ball."

I could barely make him out over the thunderous applause.

Quick hands, I repeated to myself. *Focus on form.*

I took a few practice swings and stepped one foot into the batter's box. I ignored the knots in my stomach, squared my hips toward the plate, lifted the bat, and faced the mound.

Title Game

She's going to throw a fastball right down the middle, I thought.

I swiped my forehead, worried that the sweat on my brow would drip into my eyes. With one foot still out of the box, I tried to think as a catcher. Martina would probably throw a fastball to get a sense of my arm speed. If I swung, that is.

Take the pitch, I thought. *Don't give them any information.*

I looked at Coach Kim at third, ready for her signal. She tugged her right ear—the signal to take a pitch. I exhaled, proud of myself for reading the situation correctly.

Confident in my plan, at least for the first pitch, I stepped my other foot into the batter's box. I raised my back elbow slightly and waited. Martina started her windup and released a fastball. I did nothing, letting the ball sail straight into the catcher's mitt.

"Strike one!" the umpire called.

I stepped out of the batter's box and took another practice swing.

"The count is 0-and-1 for Rana Parisi," announced Maya. "Bases loaded, two outs."

The cheers from the bleachers melted into a distant hum. I quieted my mind and became a little more comfortable at the plate. Coach Kim patted her stomach—the signal to swing away. The catcher threw the ball back to Martina. Again, I tried to think as a catcher.

It won't be a fastball again, I thought, *but she'll try to throw a strike. Maybe a breaking ball to try and trick me.*

I stepped back into the box, knowing I had to swing at anything close. Dottie, Alana, and Karla took their leads. I squared my hips and lifted the bat, digging the ball of my back foot into the dirt. Martina wound up and released her pitch.

As soon as the ball left her glove, I knew it was high. It arched into the sky over my head, forcing the catcher to jump up and bring it down before Dottie could steal home.

"Ball. High," called the umpire.

"Count moves to 1-and-1 for Rana Parisi," Maya continued her play-by-play. "Dodgers threaten from every base."

The wild pitch rattled Martina and she stepped off of the mound to compose herself. The cheers grew louder and my confidence grew stronger.

She's going to throw another fastball, I realized. *She's too scared to throw anything else now!*

Coach Kim signaled to swing away. I stepped quickly back into the box, knowing this was the moment of truth. I looked at the gap between the first and second basemen and visualized myself hitting a line drive. I remembered my form. Grip. Hand position. Swing. Contact. Follow-through.

Martina wound up for a third time and released her pitch. Just as I suspected, it hurtled straight down the middle. I kept my eye on the ball and brought my hands directly towards it. My arms followed as I shifted my weight and swung the bat.

A burst of energy zinged into my hands as the bat and ball connected. I powered through, bringing the bat around to my front shoulder for the follow-through.

"Run, Rana, run!" the crowd cheered.

The ball shot down the line. It headed straight toward the gap between first and second. I dropped the bat and ran as fast as I could.

Fighting the temptation to watch the ball, I kept my eye on Coach Lucy's baserunning directions. She waved her arms excitedly in a circle as Cardinals darted in every direction.

"Take two! Take two!" she yelled.

Maya's voice echoed across the field as I headed for second.

"One run scores!" she yelled. "The winning run heads for home!"

I looked at third, expecting to see Coach Kim. But she wasn't there! Instead, she was halfway to home, following Alana as she ran toward the plate.

I stopped at second and watched. When Alana slid home, the ball nowhere in sight, I realized what had just happened.

"Dodgers win!" Maya yelled. "Dodgers win the championship!"

Relief washed over my body and I collapsed happily onto the base. A sea of blue and yellow flooded the field. Players and fans joined together at home plate, jumping up and down in one giant victory pile.

Darius, Jasper, and Ruby ran toward the center. Mom and Dad followed close behind. I laughed as my family disappeared into the celebration.

"Last to first! Last to first!" the pile chanted.

Louie and Alana emerged from the mayhem and ran to second.

"That was incredible!" Louie screamed. "You just hit a double!"

"You did it! We did it!" Alana rejoiced.

They grabbed my hands and lifted me off the base. As we ran to join our team, I heard a different voice echo over the stadium speakers. It wasn't Maya. It was the deeper, male voice of the freckle-faced teenager recapping the final score.

In a heartbeat, I knew why. There, waiting for us at the pitcher's mound, stood Maya.

"Wahoo!" she cheered. "Congratulations!"

The four of us collided, forming our own mini victory pile. We laughed and hugged before taking seats around the pitcher's mound. I knew I would never forget this moment for as long as I lived.

"Rana," Maya yelled as she turned away from Louie, "you just batted in the winning run to win

the championship for the Dodgers! What are you going to do next?"

I looked into the faces of my dearest friends. "That's up to you, birthday girl!" I answered. "What do you say?"

Maya smiled, dropped her journal on the ground, and looked at Louie.

"Let's party!" she shouted.

ABOUT THE AUTHOR

Brigitte Cooper is a kid lit author, stripes enthusiast and all-around word nerd! She loves sports and once pitched under the bright lights when her Little League softball team, The Dodgers, made the championships! She lives in Greenwich, CT with her kind and funny husband, and enjoys visiting her hometown in Northeastern Pennsylvania. She is lucky to have amazing family, friends, and four furry sidekicks, including an orange kitty named Ginger.

ABOUT THE ILLUSTRATOR

Tim Heitz is an LA based illustrator from St. Louis, Missouri. He began doodling at age 3, went on to receive his Associate in Fine Arts from St. Louis Community College at Florissant Valley and then moved to California, where he finished his studies at San Jose State University, graduating with a Bachelors in Fine Arts (emphasis in animation/illustration). Tim then began his career as a Story Artist in Feature Animation and freelance illustrator for children's books.